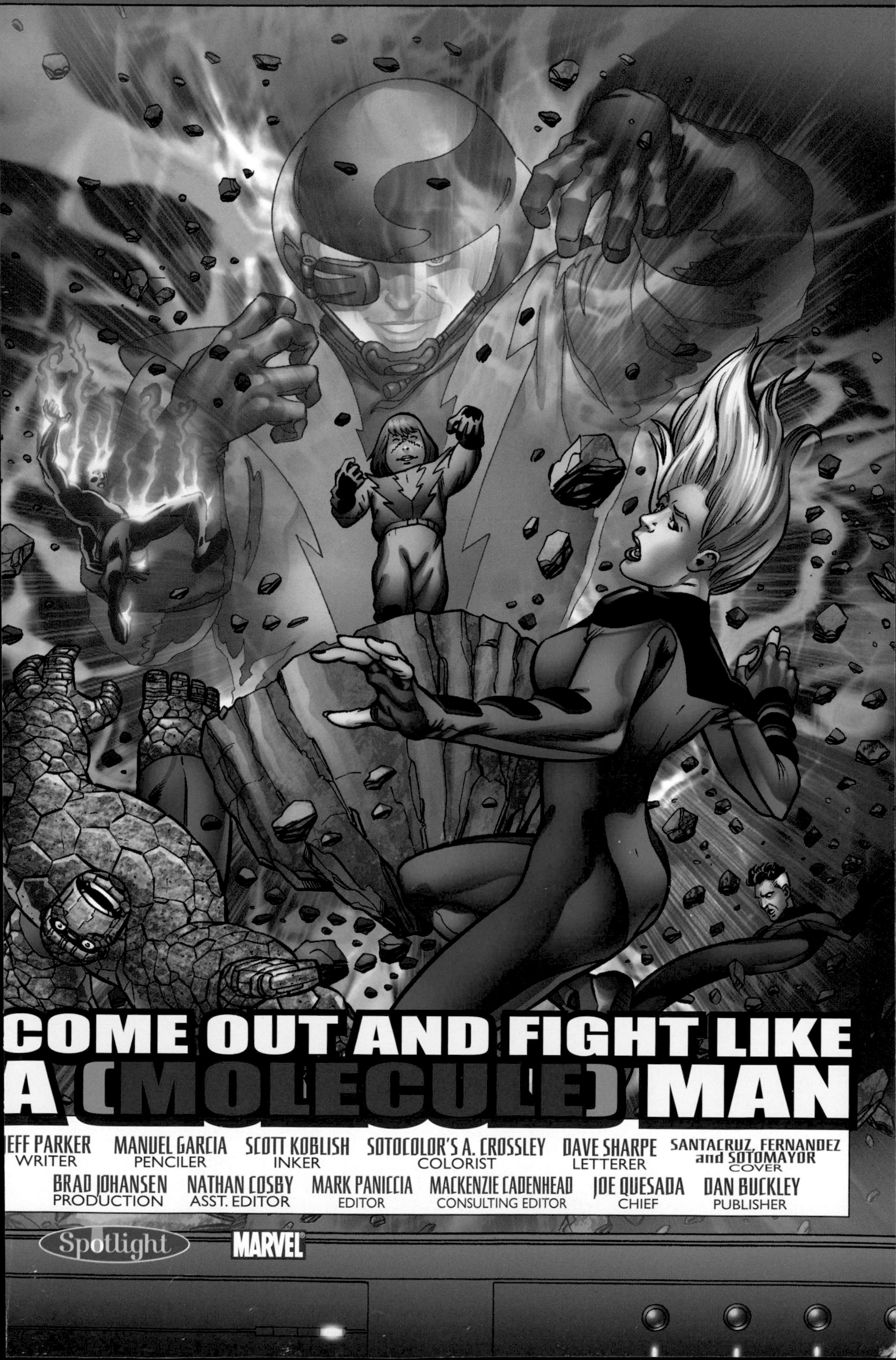

COME OUT AND FIGHT LIKE A (MOLECULE) MAN

JEFF PARKER WRITER
MANUEL GARCIA PENCILER
SCOTT KOBLISH INKER
SOTOCOLOR'S A. CROSSLEY COLORIST
DAVE SHARPE LETTERER
SANTACRUZ, FERNANDEZ and SOTOMAYOR COVER
BRAD JOHANSEN PRODUCTION
NATHAN COSBY ASST. EDITOR
MARK PANICCIA EDITOR
MACKENZIE CADENHEAD CONSULTING EDITOR
JOE QUESADA CHIEF
DAN BUCKLEY PUBLISHER

Spotlight MARVEL

VISIT US AT
www.abdopublishing.com

Reinforced library bound edition published in 2008 by Spotlight, a division of the ABDO Publishing Group, 8000 West 78th Street, Edina, Minnesota 55439. Spotlight produces high-quality reinforced library bound editions for schools and libraries. Published by agreement with Marvel Characters, Inc.

Library of Congress Cataloging-in-Publication Data

Parker, Jeff, 1966-
  Come out and fight like a (molecule) man / Jeff Parker, writer ; Manuel Garcia, penciler ; Scott Koblish, inker ; A. Crossley, colorist ; Dave Sharpe, letterer ; Santacruz, Fernandez and Sotomayor, cover. -- Reinforced library bound ed.
      p. cm. -- (Fantastic Four)
  "Marvel age"--Cover.
  Revision of issue 11 of Marvel adventures Fantastic Four.
  ISBN 978-1-59961-388-8
  1. Graphic novels. I. Garcia, Manuel. II. Marvel adventures Fantastic Four. 11. III. Title.

PN6728.F33P34 2008
741.5'973--dc22

                                                      2007020253

All Spotlight books have reinforced library bindings and are manufactured in the United States of America.

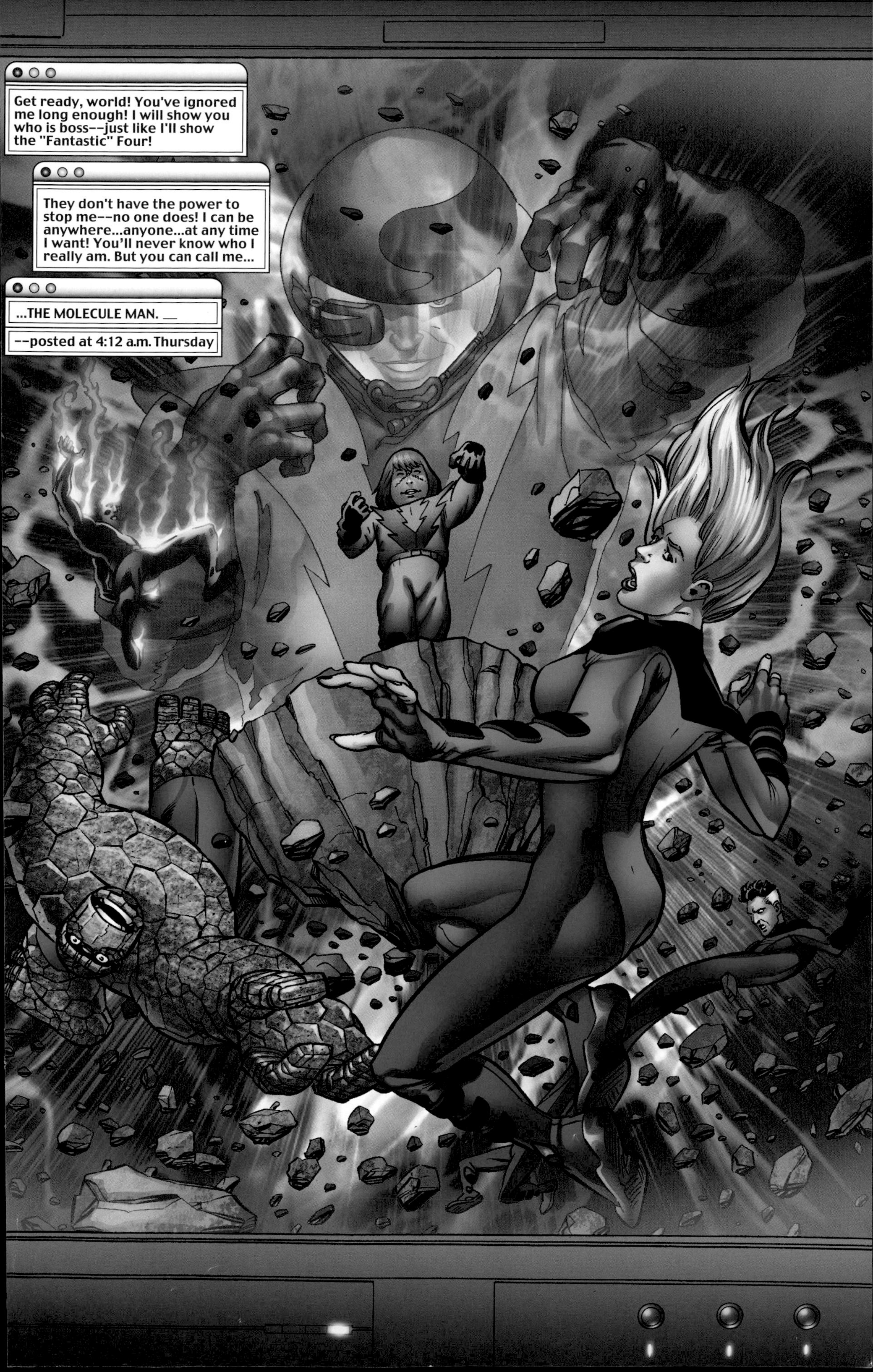
Get ready, world! You've ignored me long enough! I will show you who is boss--just like I'll show the "Fantastic" Four!
They don't have the power to stop me--no one does! I can be anywhere...anyone...at any time I want! You'll never know who I really am. But you can call me...
...THE MOLECULE MAN.
--posted at 4:12 a.m. Thursday

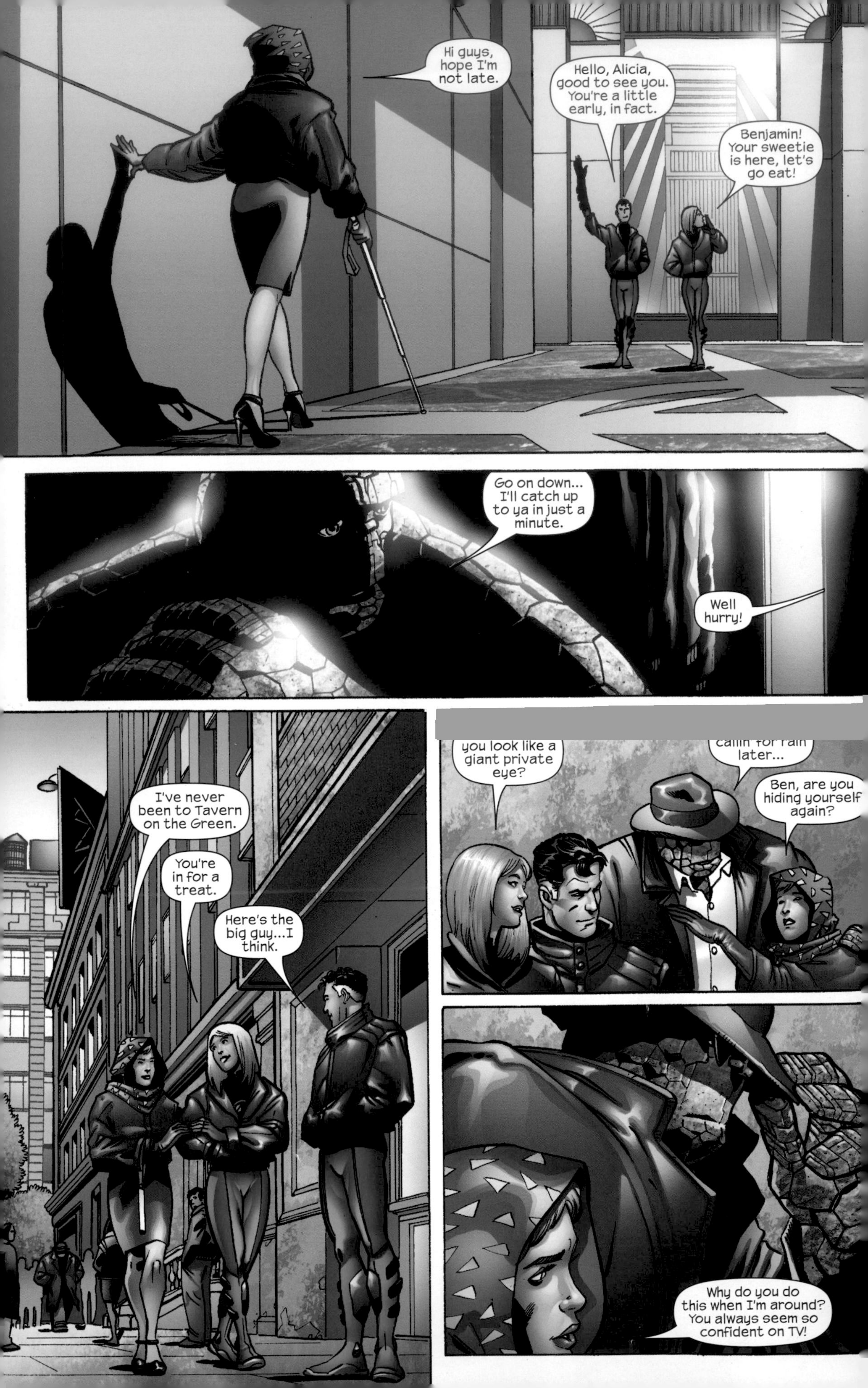

Hi guys, hope I'm not late.
Hello, Alicia, good to see you. You're a little early, in fact.
Benjamin! Your sweetie is here, let's go eat!
Go on down... I'll catch up to ya in just a minute.
Well hurry!
I've never been to Tavern on the Green.
You're in for a treat.
Here's the big guy...I think.
you look like a giant private eye?
later...
Ben, are you hiding yourself again?
Why do you do this when I'm around? You always seem so confident on TV!

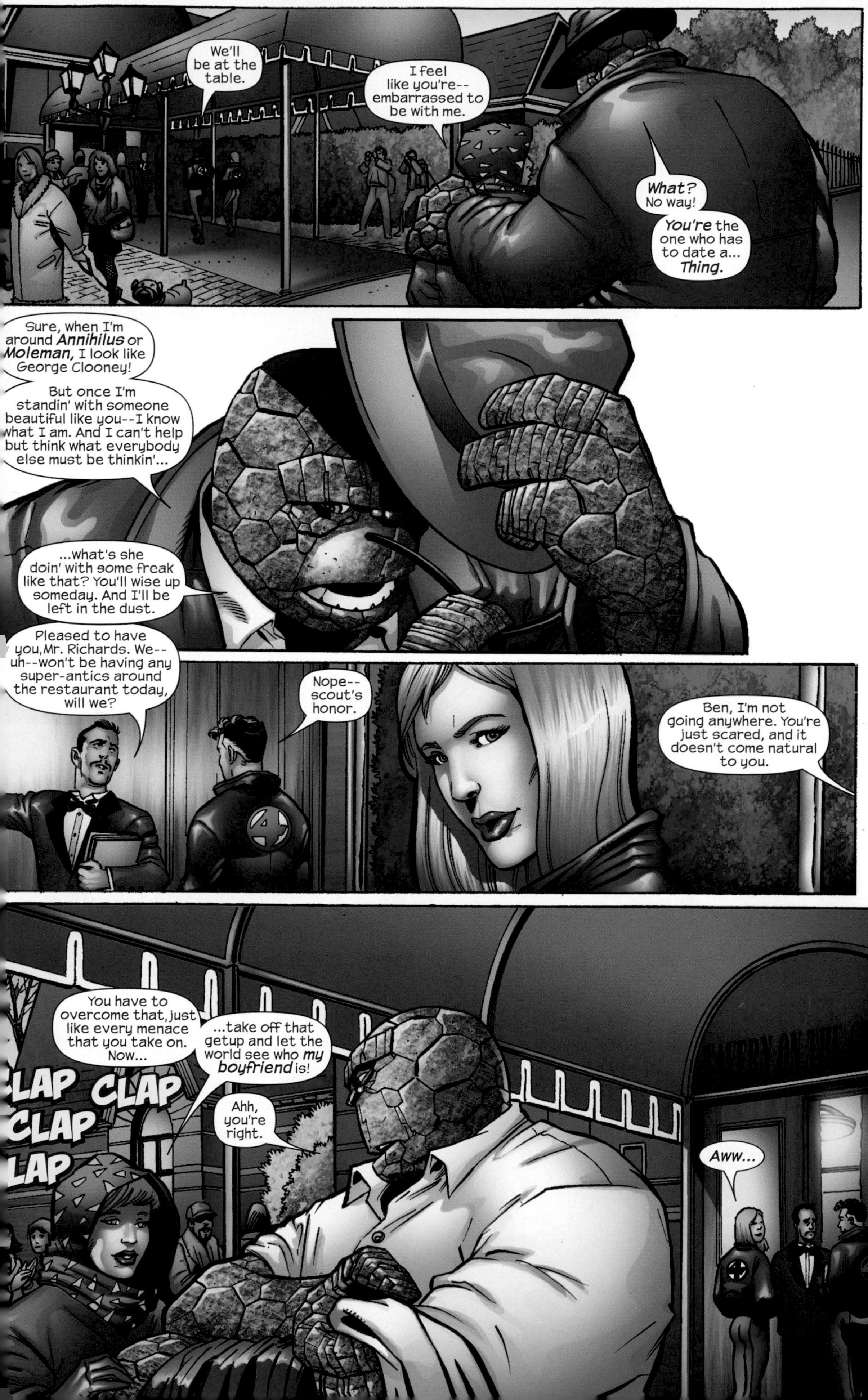
We'll be at the table.
I feel like you're-- embarrassed to be with me.
What? No way!
You're the one who has to date a... Thing.
Sure, when I'm around Annihilus or Moleman, I look like George Clooney!
But once I'm standin' with someone beautiful like you--I know what I am. And I can't help but think what everybody else must be thinkin'...
...what's she doin' with some freak like that? You'll wise up someday. And I'll be left in the dust.
Pleased to have you, Mr. Richards. We-- uh--won't be having any super-antics around the restaurant today, will we?
Nope-- scout's honor.
Ben, I'm not going anywhere. You're just scared, and it doesn't come natural to you.
You have to overcome that, just like every menace that you take on. Now...
...take off that getup and let the world see who my boyfriend is!
Ahh, you're right.
CLAP CLAP CLAP LAP
Aww...

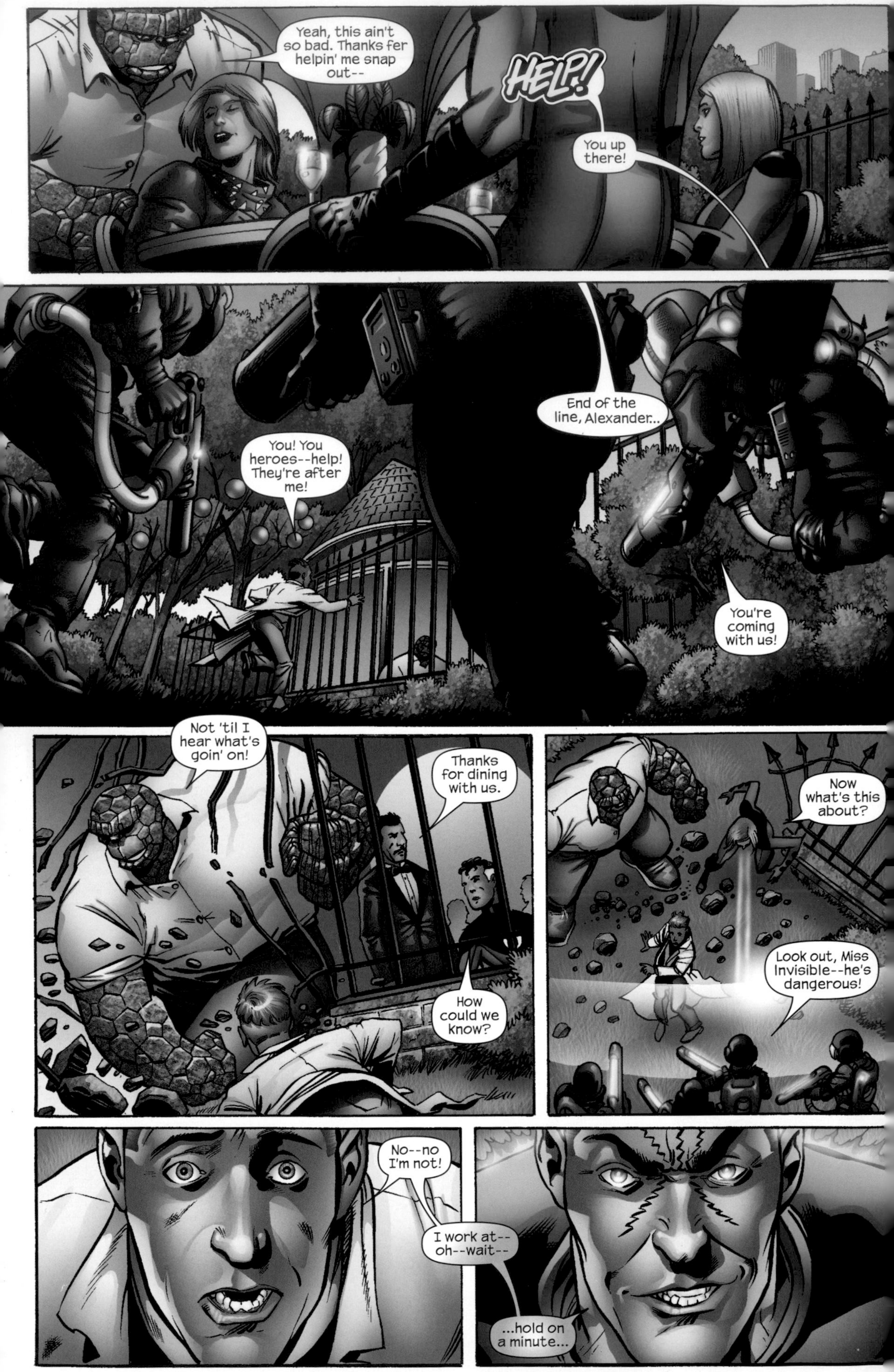
Yeah, this ain't so bad. Thanks fer helpin' me snap out--
HELP!
You up there!
End of the line, Alexander...
You! You heroes--help! They're after me!
You're coming with us!
Not 'til I hear what's goin' on!
Thanks for dining with us.
How could we know?
Now what's this about?
Look out, Miss Invisible--he's dangerous!
No--no I'm not!
I work at-- oh--wait--
...hold on a minute...

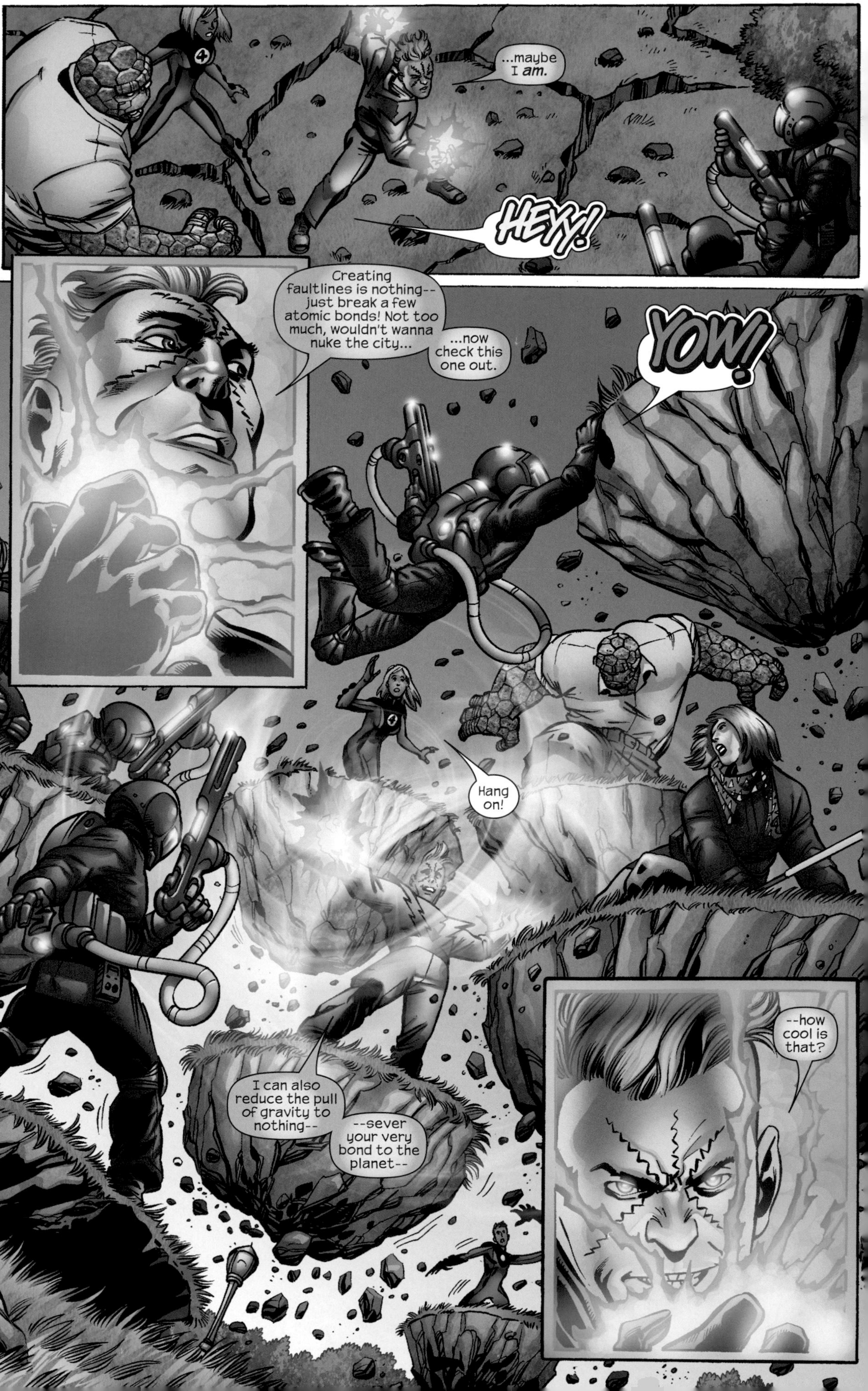
...maybe I *am*.
HEYY!
Creating faultlines is nothing-- just break a few atomic bonds! Not too much, wouldn't wanna nuke the city...
...now check this one out.
YOW!
Hang on!
I can also reduce the pull of gravity to nothing--
--sever your very bond to the planet--
--how cool is that?

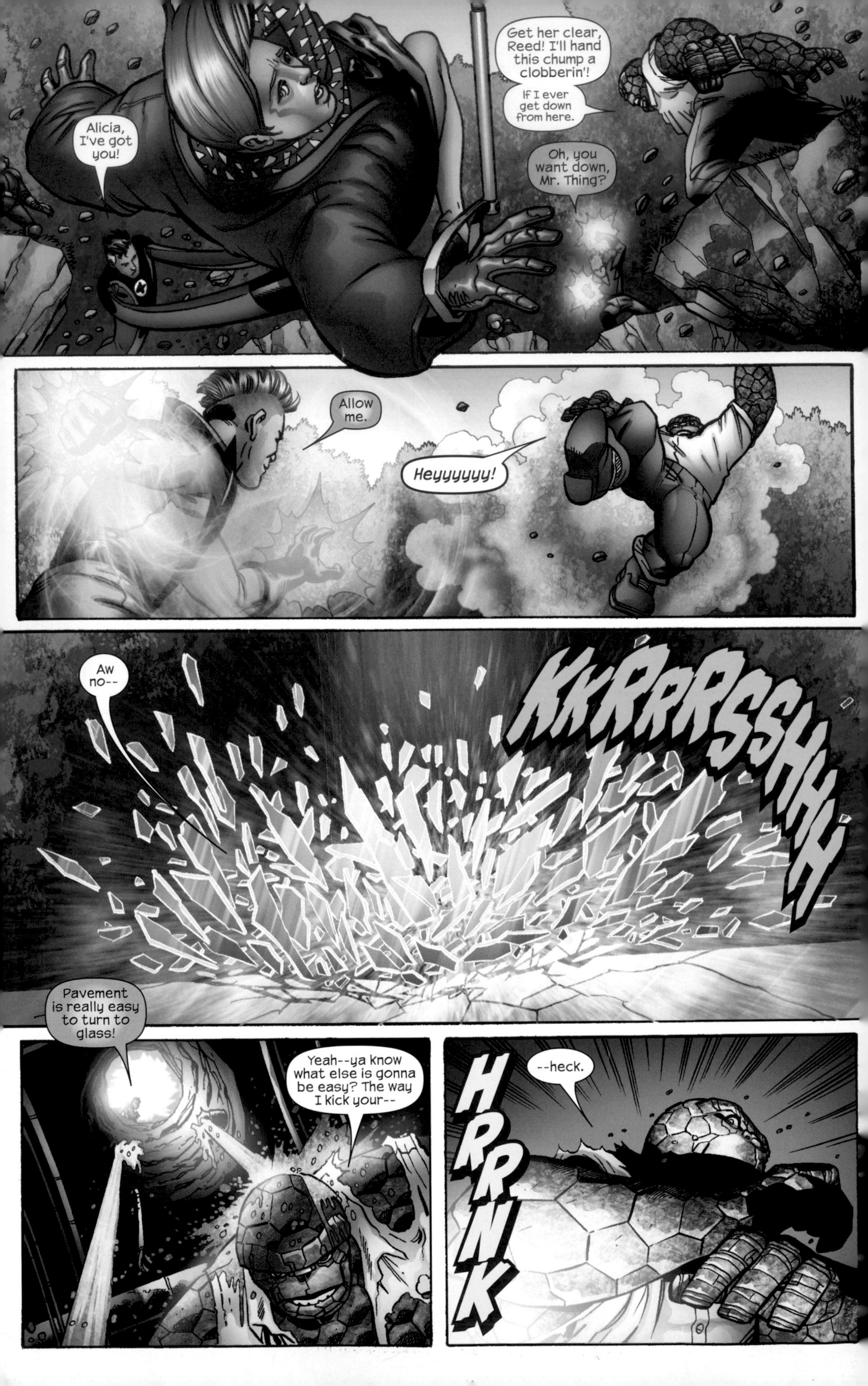
Alicia, I've got you!
Get her clear, Reed! I'll hand this chump a clobberin'!
If I ever get down from here.
Oh, you want down, Mr. Thing?
Allow me.
Heyyyyyy!
Aw no--
KKRRRSSHHH
Pavement is really easy to turn to glass!
Yeah--ya know what else is gonna be easy? The way I kick your--
HRRNK
--heck.

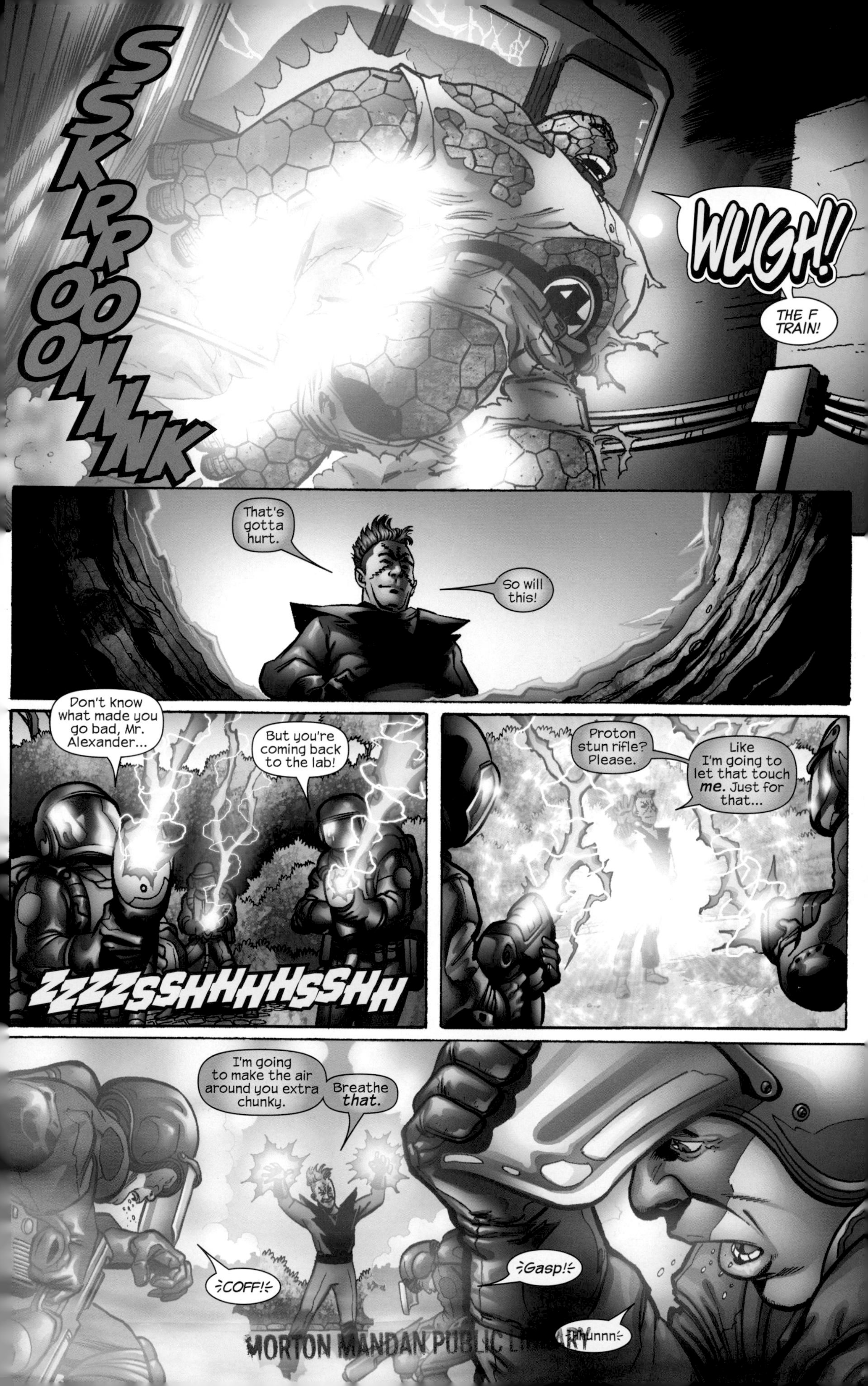
SSKRROOONNNK
WUGH!
THE F TRAIN!
That's gotta hurt.
So will this!
Don't know what made you go bad, Mr. Alexander...
But you're coming back to the lab!
ZZZZSSHHHHHSSHH
Proton stun rifle? Please.
Like I'm going to let that touch *me*. Just for that...
I'm going to make the air around you extra chunky.
Breathe *that*.
COFF!
Gasp!
Hhunnn

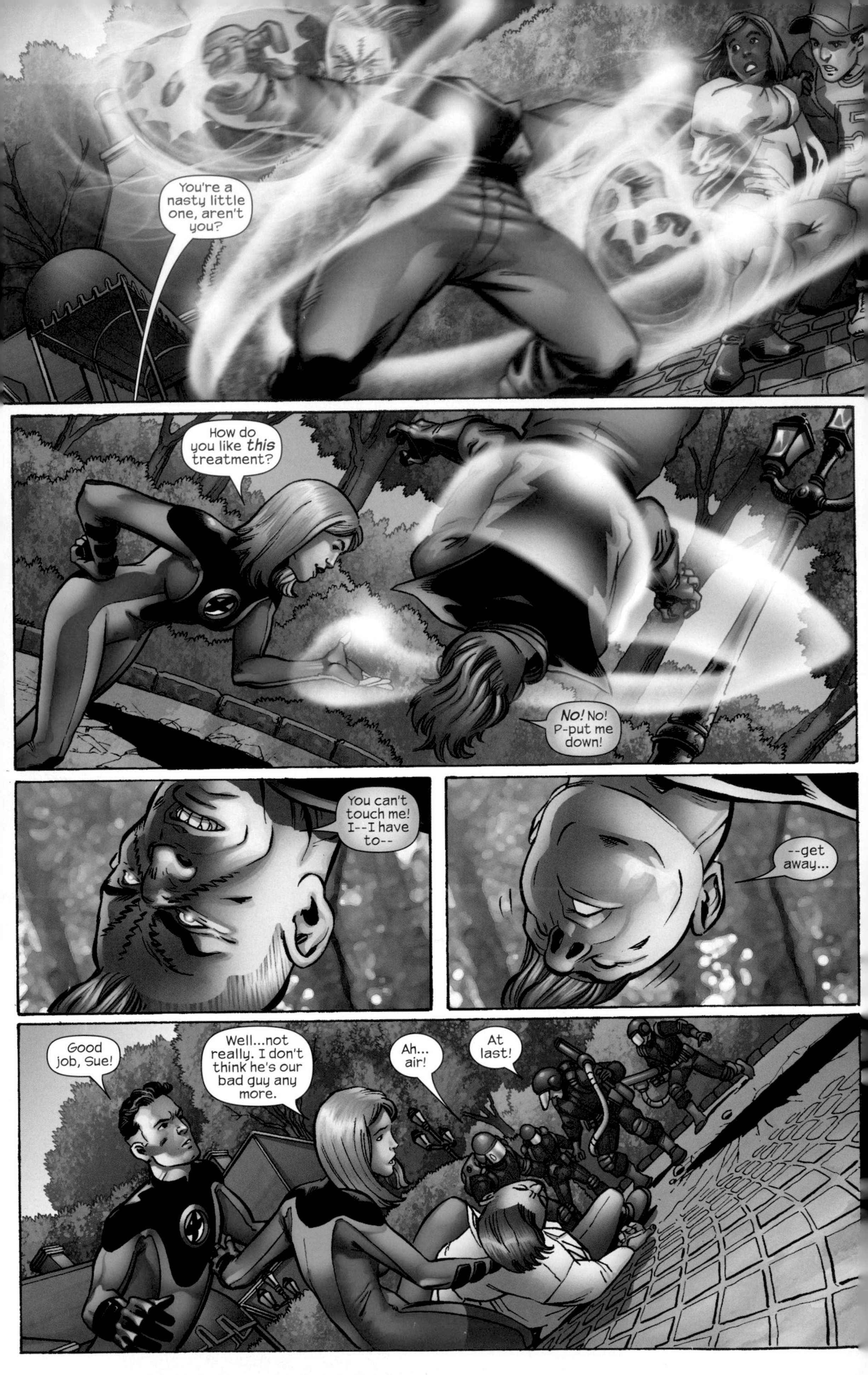
You're a nasty little one, aren't you?
How do you like *this* treatment?
No! No! P-put me down!
You can't touch me! I--I have to--
--get away...
Good job, Sue!
Well...not really. I don't think he's our bad guy any more.
Ah... air!
At last!

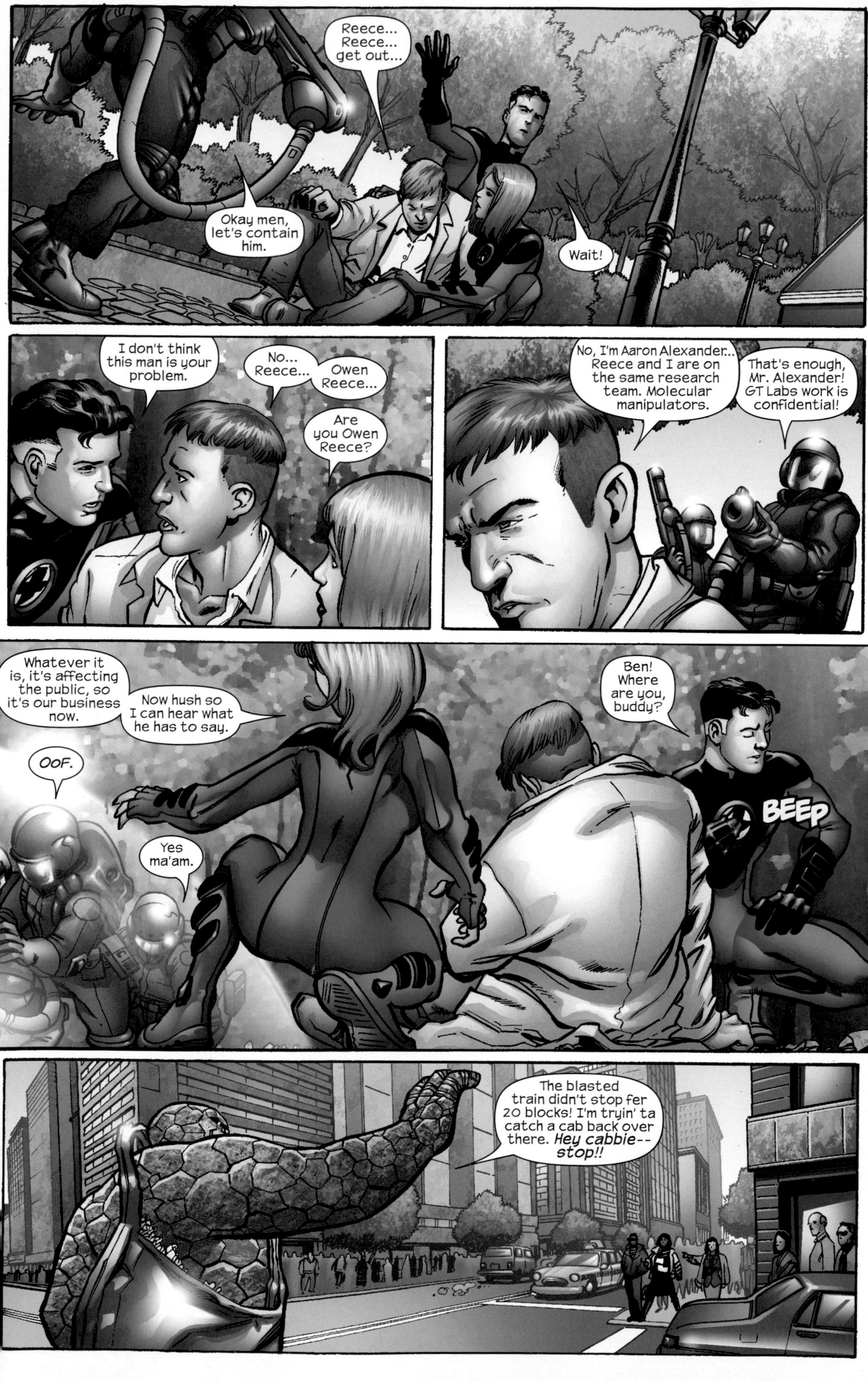
Reece... Reece... get out...
Okay men, let's contain him.
Wait!
I don't think this man is your problem.
No... Reece...
Owen Reece...
Are you Owen Reece?
No, I'm Aaron Alexander... Reece and I are on the same research team. Molecular manipulators.
That's enough, Mr. Alexander! GT Labs work is confidential!
Whatever it is, it's affecting the public, so it's our business now.
Now hush so I can hear what he has to say.
OOF.
Yes ma'am.
Ben! Where are you, buddy?
BEEP
The blasted train didn't stop fer 20 blocks! I'm tryin' ta catch a cab back over there. *Hey cabbie-- stop!!*

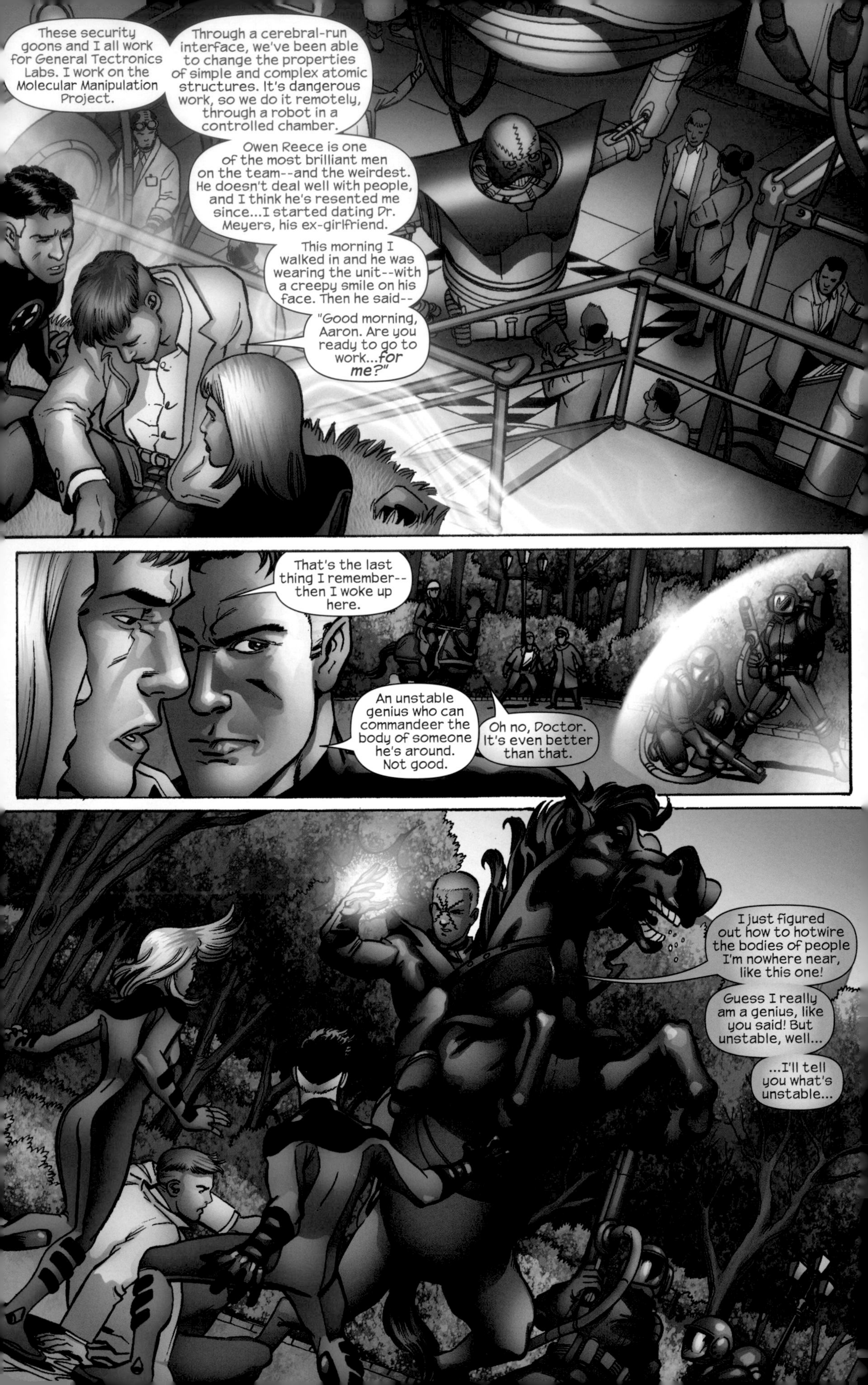
These security goons and I all work for General Tectronics Labs. I work on the Molecular Manipulation Project.
Through a cerebral-run interface, we've been able to change the properties of simple and complex atomic structures. It's dangerous work, so we do it remotely, through a robot in a controlled chamber.
Owen Reece is one of the most brilliant men on the team--and the weirdest. He doesn't deal well with people, and I think he's resented me since...I started dating Dr. Meyers, his ex-girlfriend.
This morning I walked in and he was wearing the unit--with a creepy smile on his face. Then he said--
"Good morning, Aaron. Are you ready to go to work...*for me?*"
That's the last thing I remember--then I woke up here.
An unstable genius who can commandeer the body of someone he's around. Not good.
Oh no, Doctor. It's even better than that.
I just figured out how to hotwire the bodies of people I'm nowhere near, like this one!
Guess I really am a genius, like you said! But unstable, well...
...I'll tell you what's unstable...

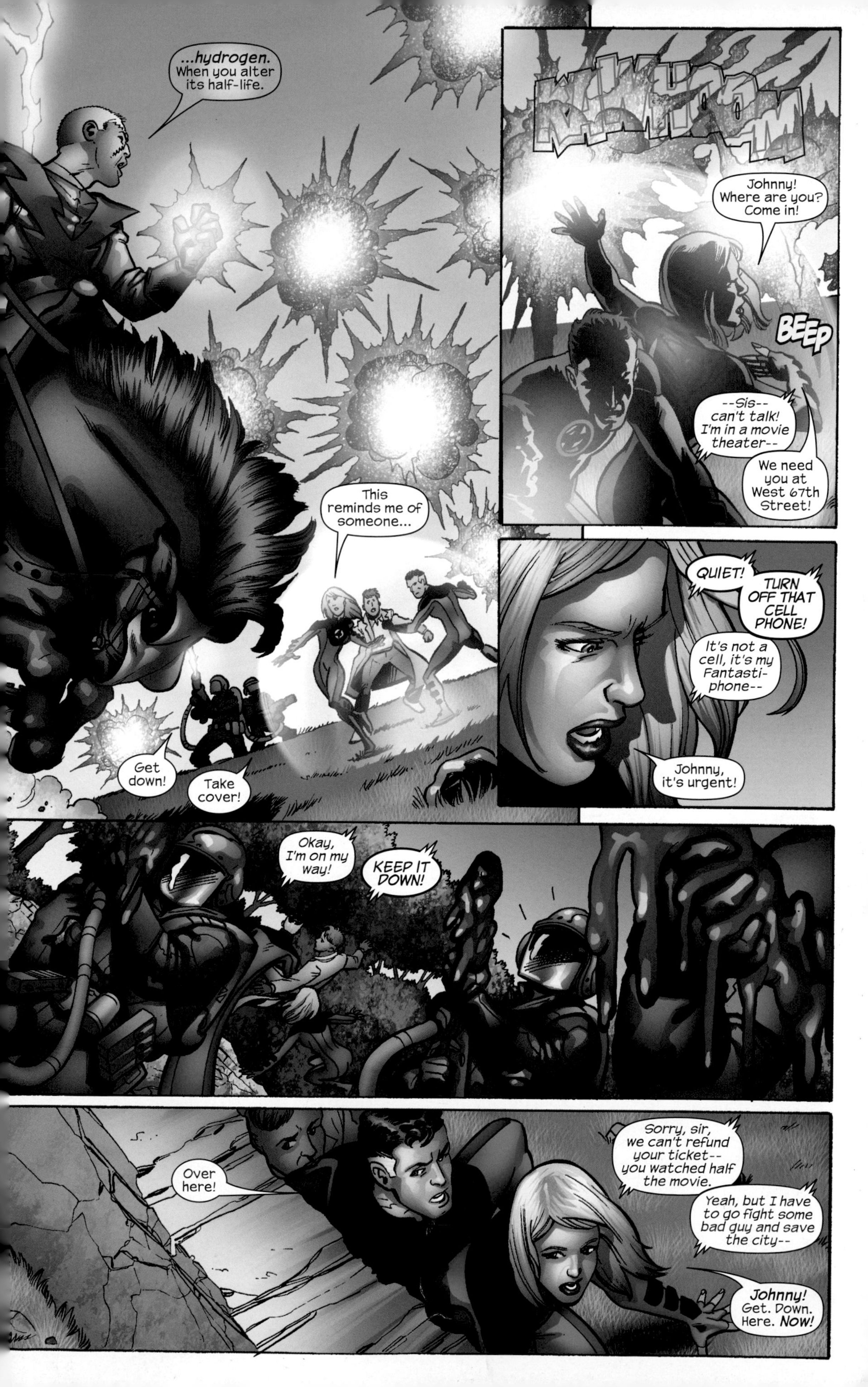

...hydrogen. When you alter its half-life.
This reminds me of someone...
Get down!
Take cover!
Johnny! Where are you? Come in!
BEEP
--Sis-- can't talk! I'm in a movie theater--
We need you at West 67th Street!
QUIET!
TURN OFF THAT CELL PHONE!
It's not a cell, it's my Fantastiphone--
Johnny, it's urgent!
Okay, I'm on my way!
KEEP IT DOWN!
Over here!
Sorry, sir, we can't refund your ticket-- you watched half the movie.
Yeah, but I have to go fight some bad guy and save the city--
Johnny! Get. Down. Here. NOW!

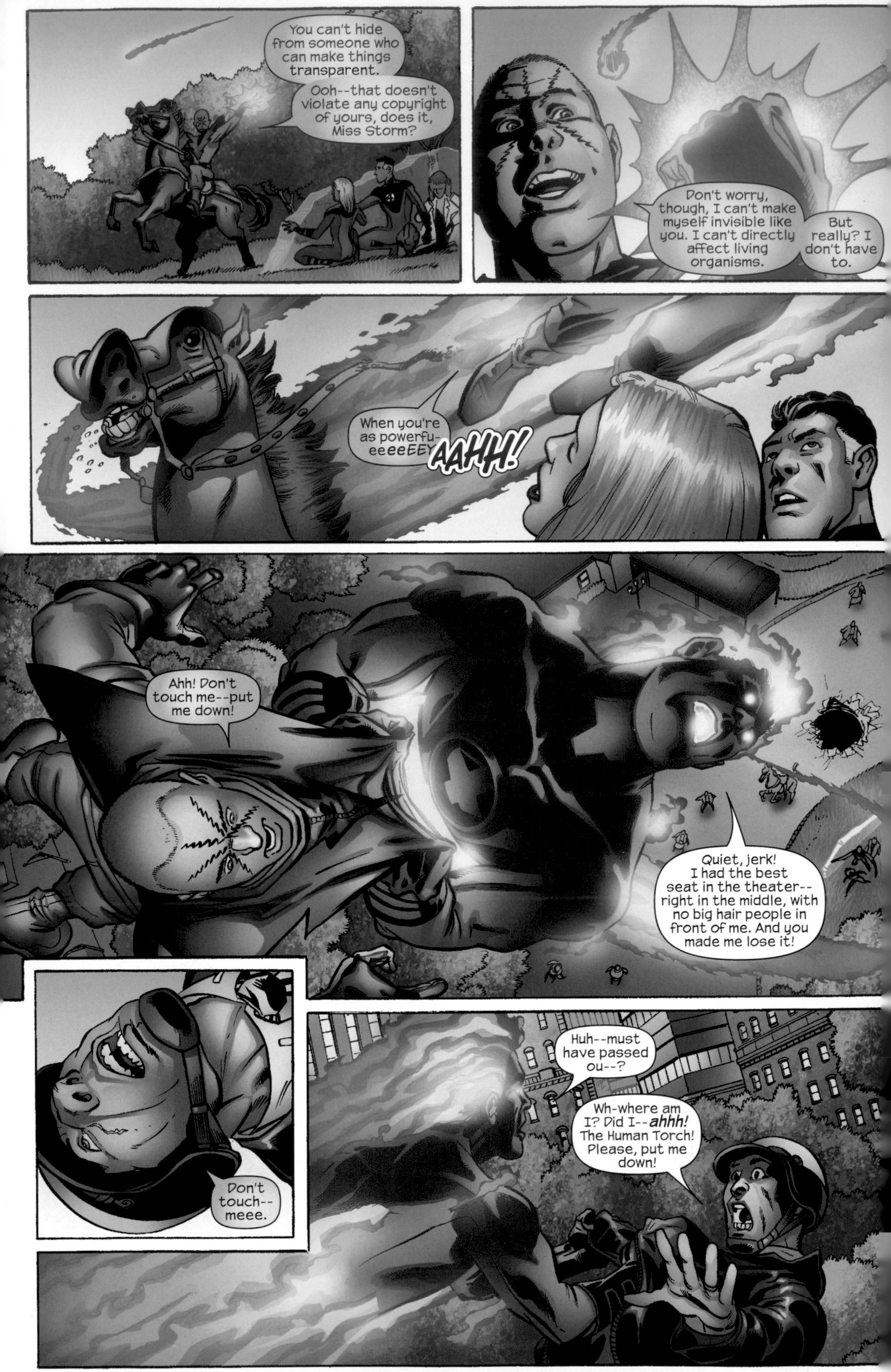
You can't hide from someone who can make things transparent.
Ooh--that doesn't violate any copyright of yours, does it, Miss Storm?
Don't worry, though, I can't make myself invisible like you. I can't directly affect living organisms.
But really? I don't have to.
When you're as powerfu-eeeeEEY
AAHH!
Ahh! Don't touch me--put me down!
Quiet, jerk! I had the best seat in the theater--right in the middle, with no big hair people in front of me. And you made me lose it!
Don't touch--meee.
Huh--must have passed ou--?
Wh-where am I? Did I--ahhh! The Human Torch! Please, put me down!

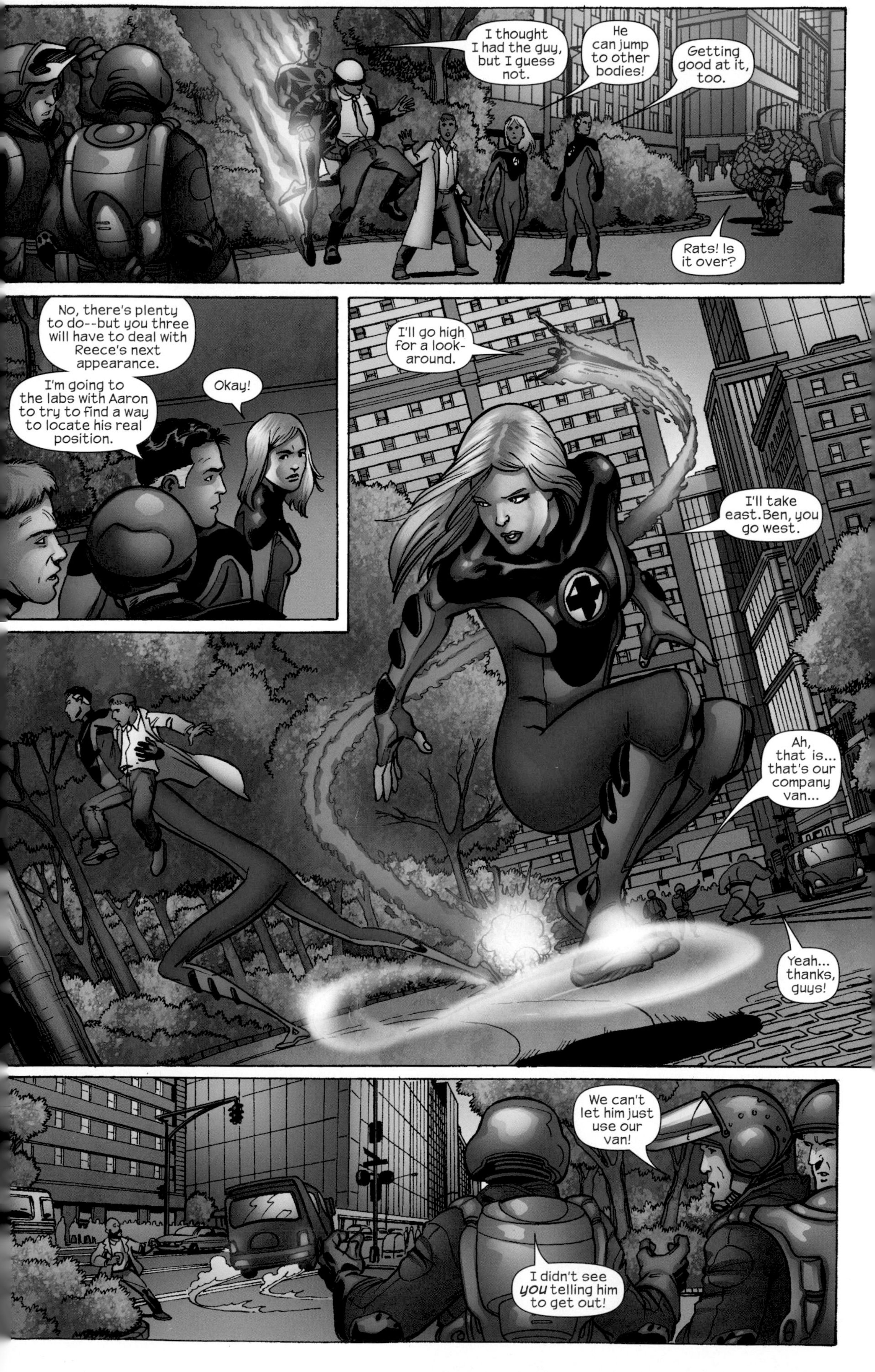
I thought I had the guy, but I guess not.
He can jump to other bodies!
Getting good at it, too.
Rats! Is it over?
No, there's plenty to do--but you three will have to deal with Reece's next appearance.
I'm going to the labs with Aaron to try to find a way to locate his real position.
Okay!
I'll go high for a look-around.
I'll take east. Ben, you go west.
Ah, that is... that's our company van...
Yeah... thanks, guys!
We can't let him just use our van!
I didn't see *you* telling him to get out!

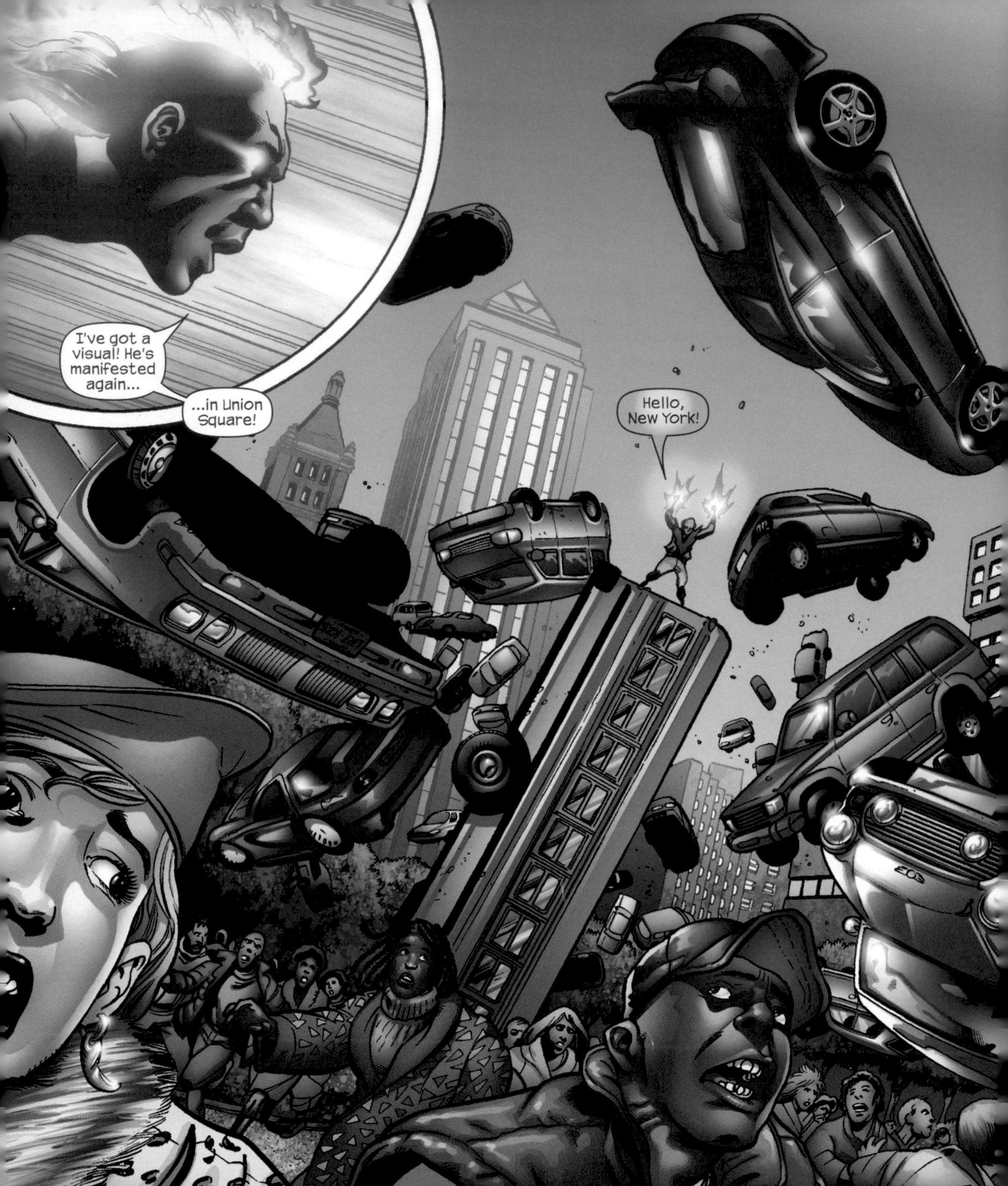
I've got a visual! He's manifested again...
...in Union Square!
Hello, New York!
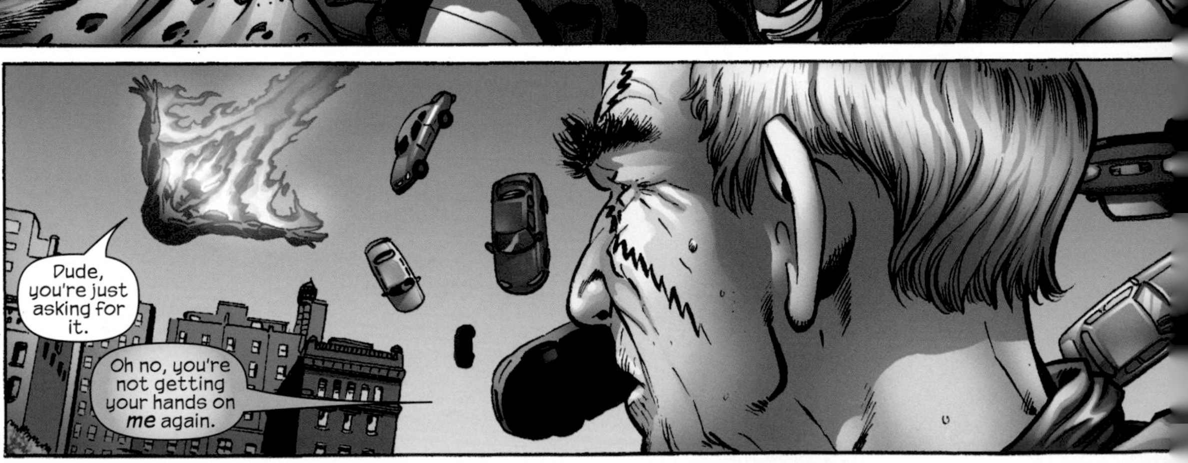
Dude, you're just asking for it.
Oh no, you're not getting your hands on *me* again.

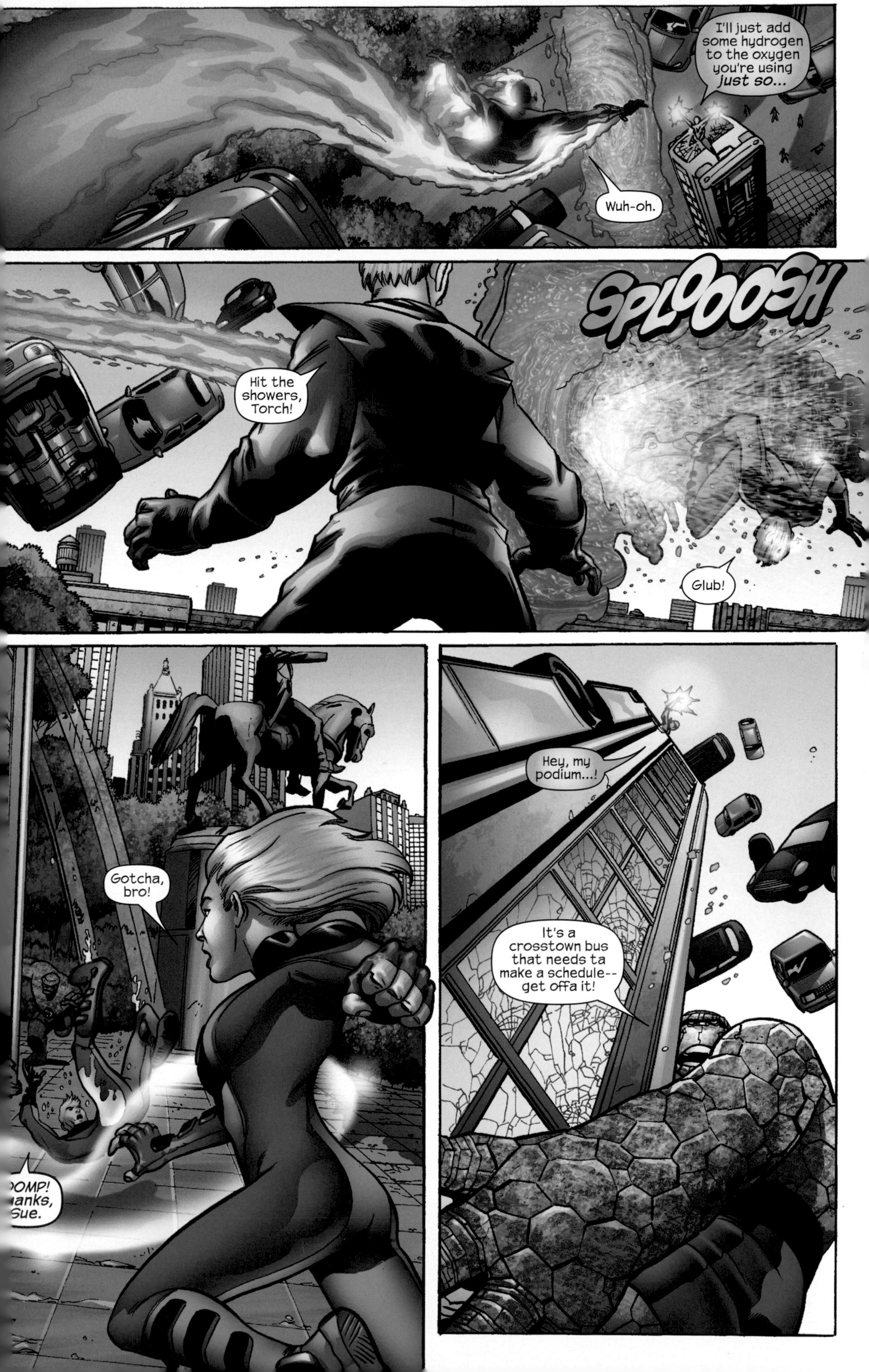
I'll just add some hydrogen to the oxygen you're using just so...
Wuh-oh.
SPLOOOSH
Hit the showers, Torch!
Glub!
Gotcha, bro!
OOMP! hanks, Sue.
Hey, my podium...!
It's a crosstown bus that needs ta make a schedule--get offa it!

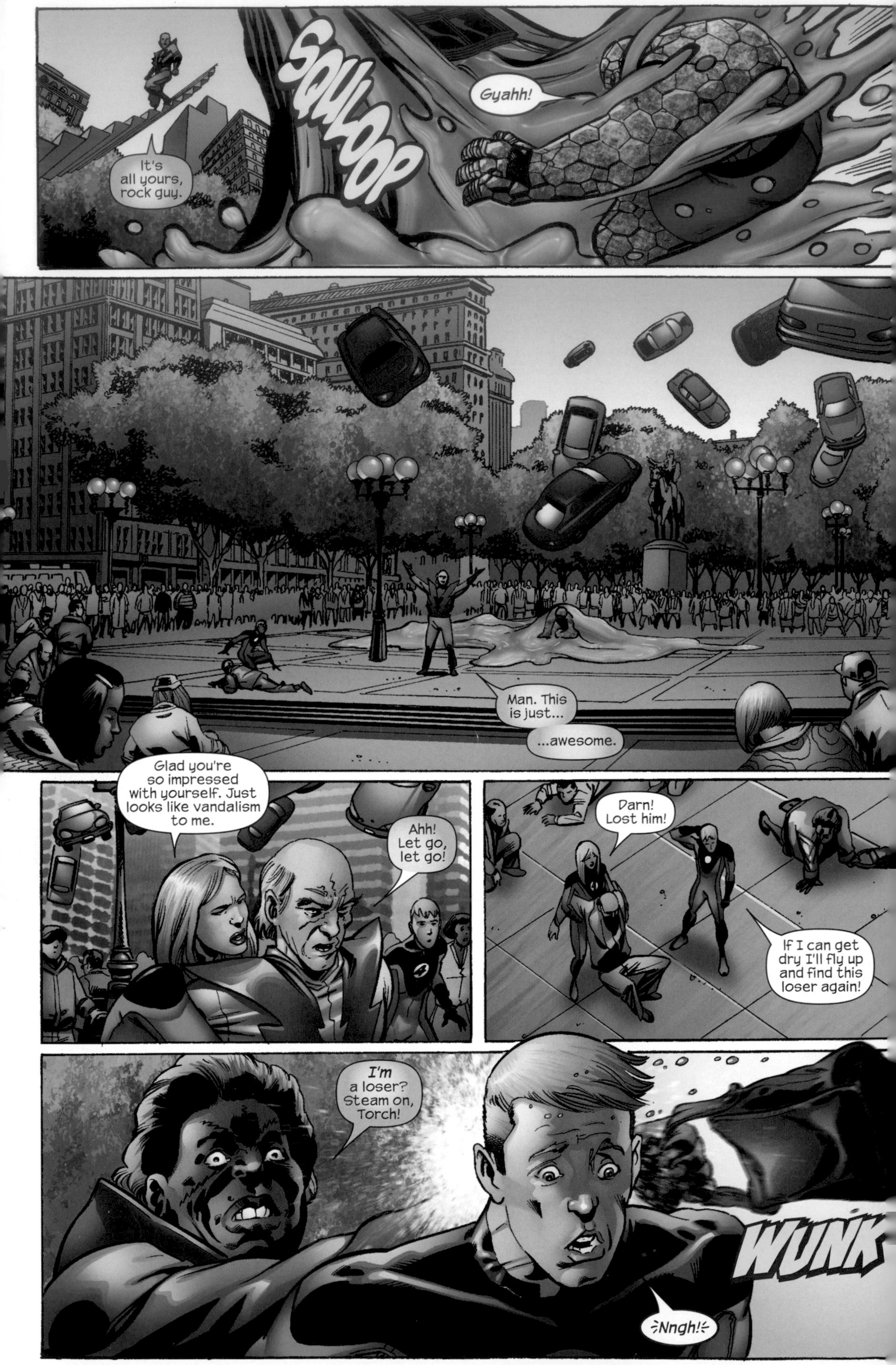
SQULOOP
Gyahh!
It's all yours, rock guy.
Man. This is just...
...awesome.
Glad you're so impressed with yourself. Just looks like vandalism to me.
Ahh! Let go, let go!
Darn! Lost him!
If I can get dry I'll fly up and find this loser again!
I'm a loser? Steam on, Torch!
WUNK
Nngh!

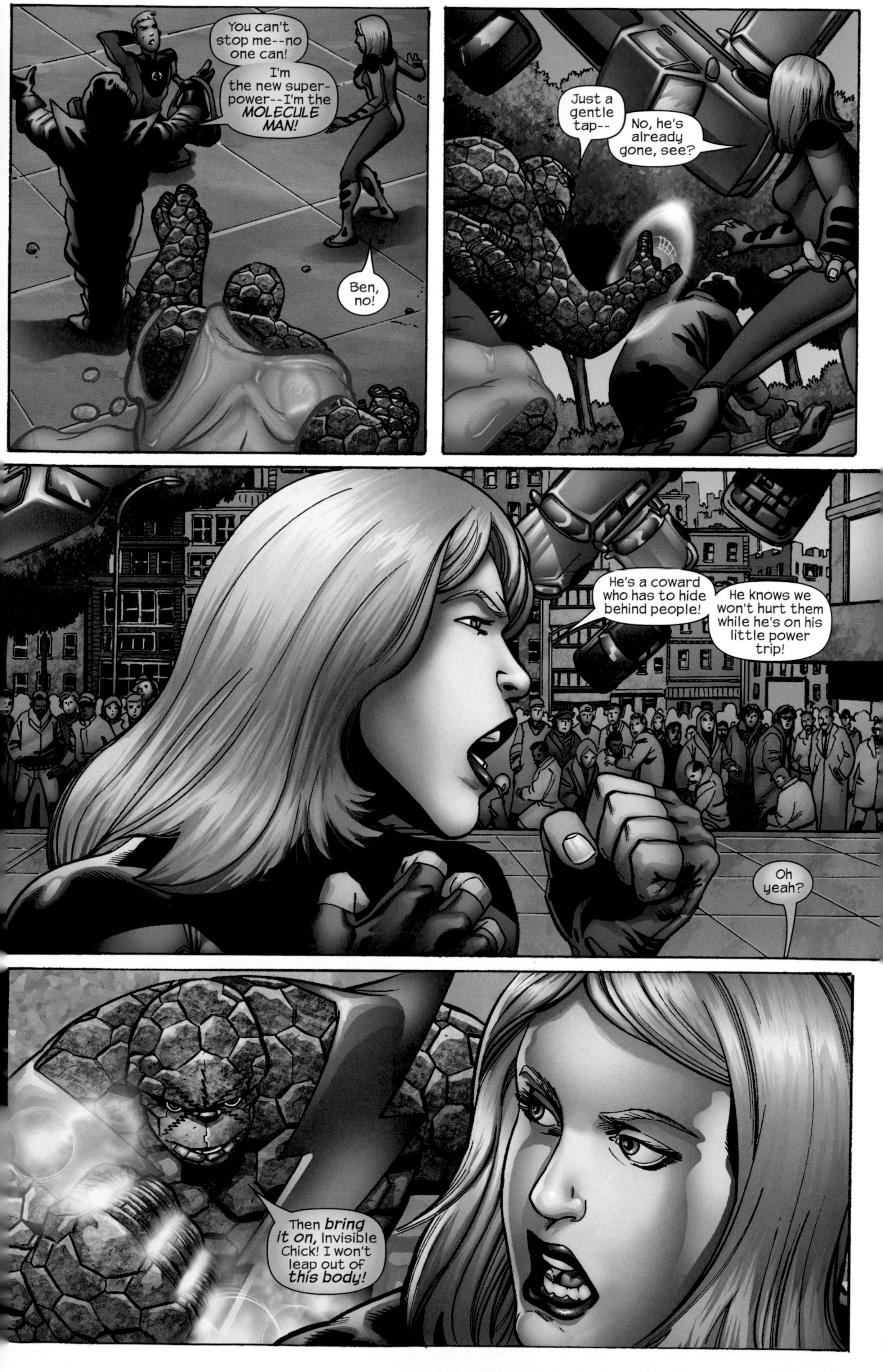
You can't stop me--no one can!
I'm the new super-power--I'm the MOLECULE MAN!
Ben, no!
Just a gentle tap--
No, he's already gone, see?
He's a coward who has to hide behind people!
He knows we won't hurt them while he's on his little power trip!
Oh yeah?
Then bring it on, Invisible Chick! I won't leap out of this body!

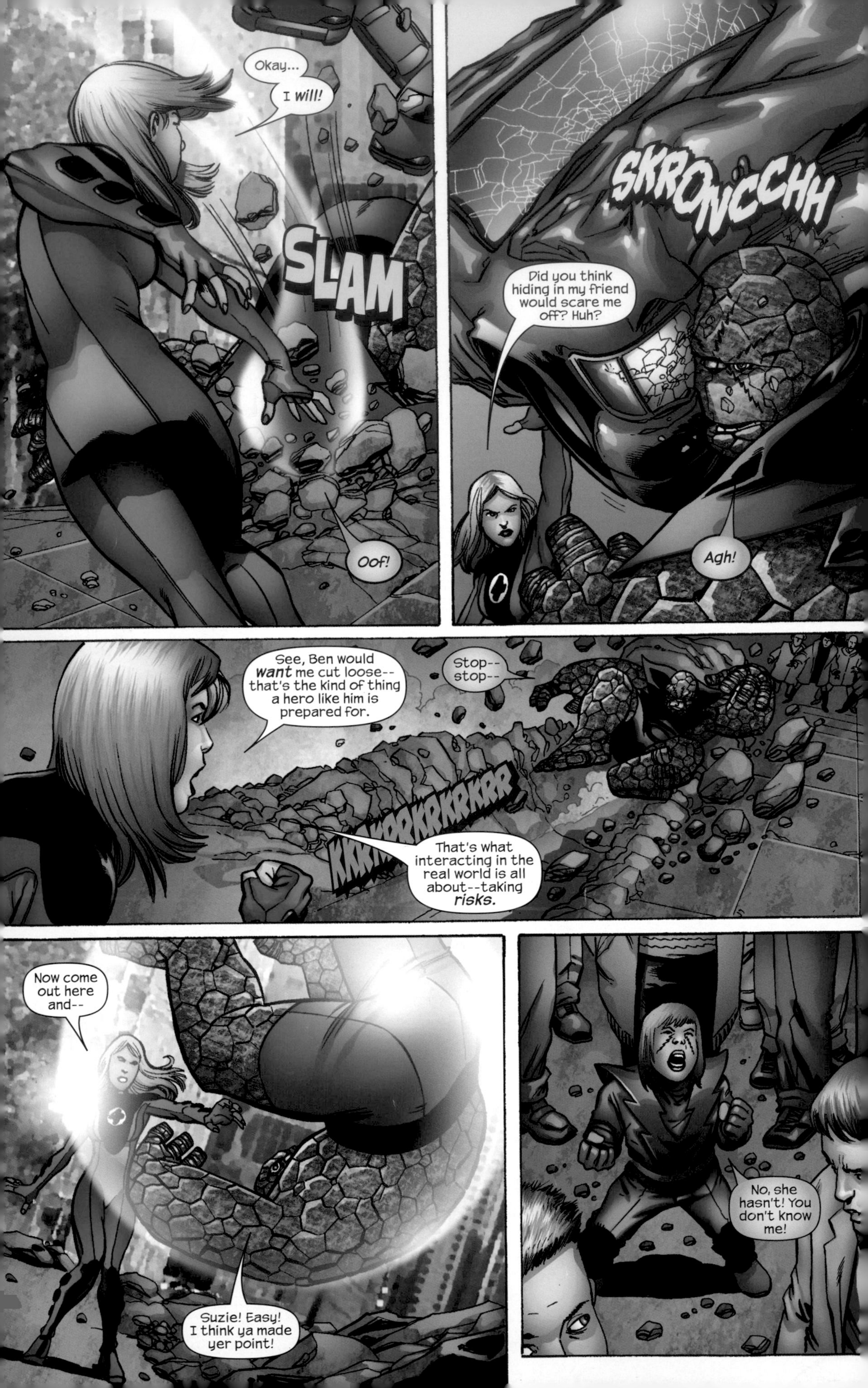
Okay...
I will!
SLAM
Oof!
SKRONCCHH
Did you think hiding in my friend would scare me off? Huh?
Agh!
See, Ben would want me cut loose--that's the kind of thing a hero like him is prepared for.
Stop--stop--
That's what interacting in the real world is all about--taking risks.
Now come out here and--
Suzie! Easy! I think ya made yer point!
No, she hasn't! You don't know me!

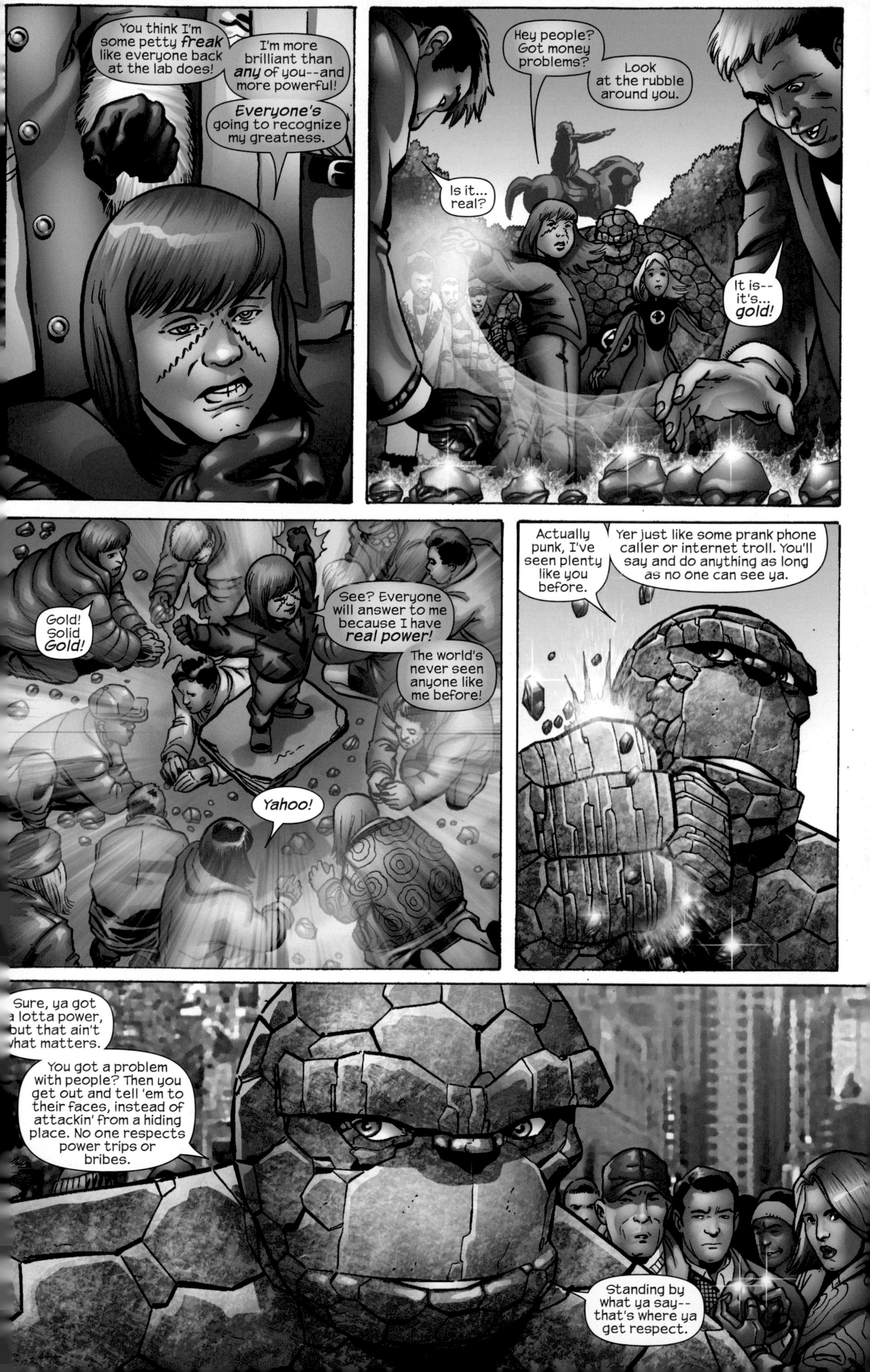
You think I'm some petty freak like everyone back at the lab does!
I'm more brilliant than any of you--and more powerful!
Everyone's going to recognize my greatness.
Hey people? Got money problems?
Look at the rubble around you.
Is it... real?
It is-- it's... gold!
Gold! Solid Gold!
See? Everyone will answer to me because I have real power!
The world's never seen anyone like me before!
Yahoo!
Actually punk, I've seen plenty like you before.
Yer just like some prank phone caller or internet troll. You'll say and do anything as long as no one can see ya.
Sure, ya got a lotta power, but that ain't what matters.
You got a problem with people? Then you get out and tell 'em to their faces, instead of attackin' from a hiding place. No one respects power trips or bribes.
Standing by what ya say-- that's where ya get respect.

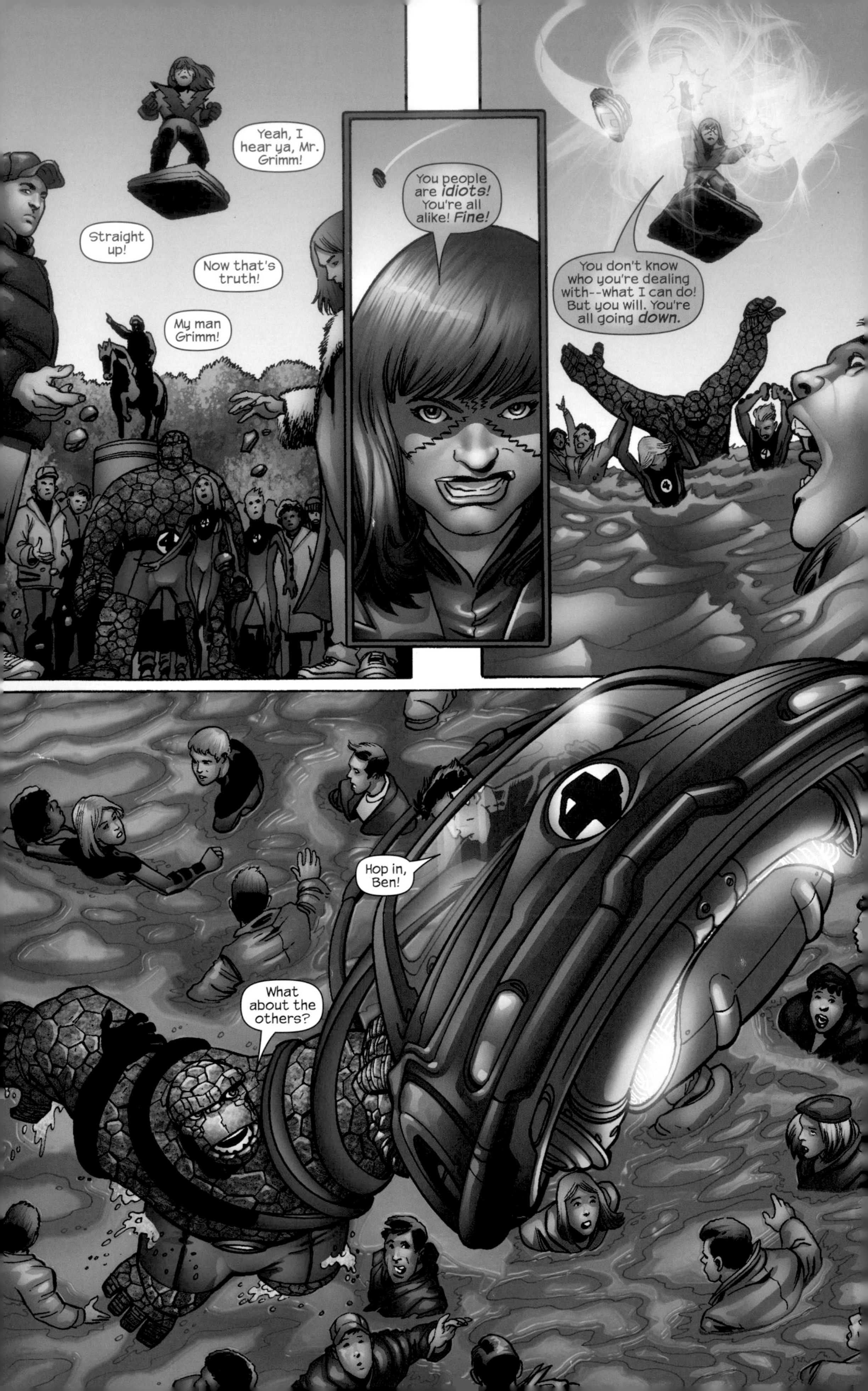
Yeah, I hear ya, Mr. Grimm!
Straight up!
Now that's truth!
My man Grimm!
You people are idiots! You're all alike! Fine!
You don't know who you're dealing with--what I can do! But you will. You're all going down.
Hop in, Ben!
What about the others?

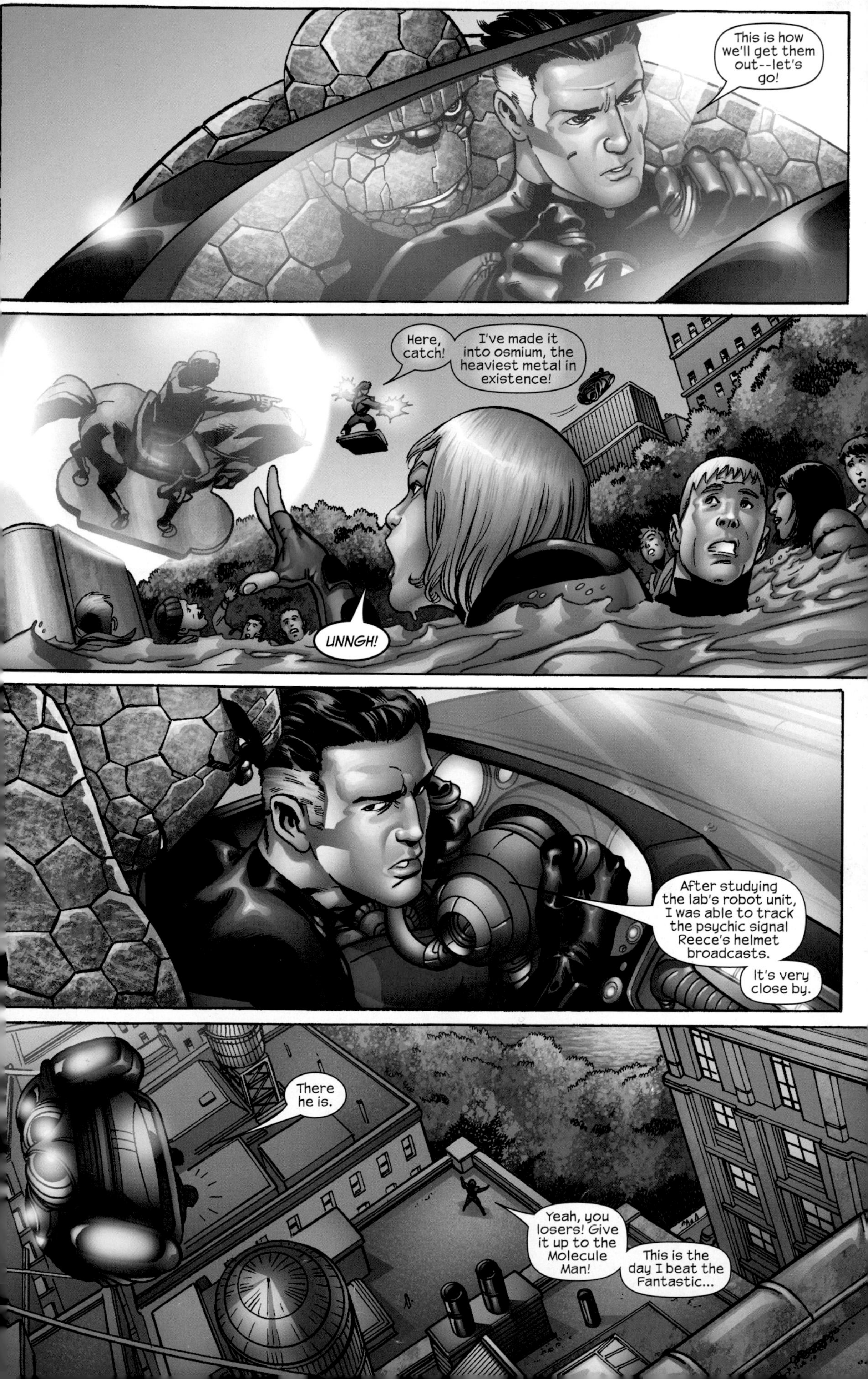
This is how we'll get them out--let's go!
Here, catch!
I've made it into osmium, the heaviest metal in existence!
UNNGH!
After studying the lab's robot unit, I was able to track the psychic signal Reece's helmet broadcasts.
It's very close by.
There he is.
Yeah, you losers! Give it up to the Molecule Man!
This is the day I beat the Fantastic...

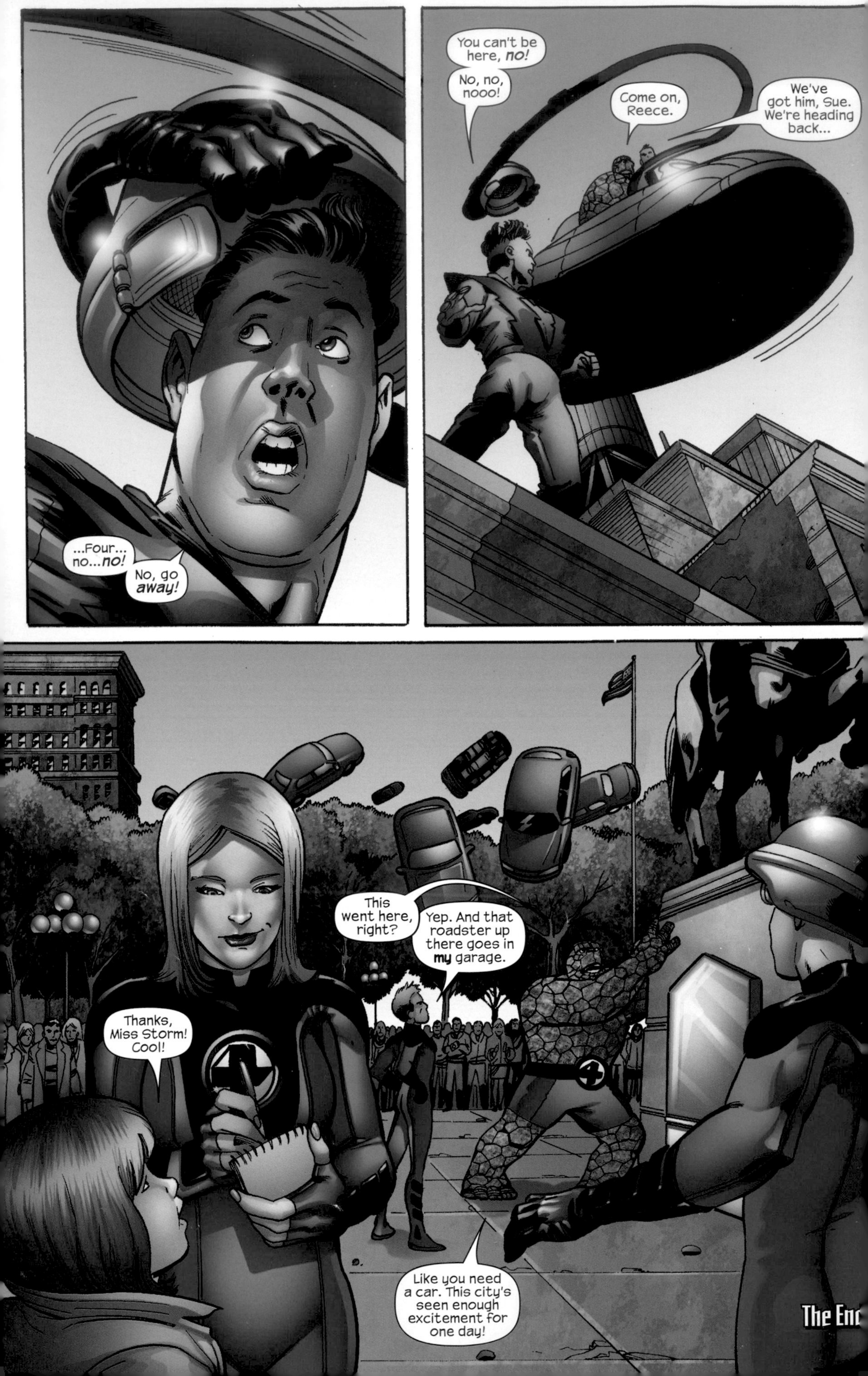

...Four... no...*no!*
No, go *away!*
You can't be here, *no!*
No, no, nooo!
Come on, Reece.
We've got him, Sue. We're heading back...
This went here, right?
Yep. And that roadster up there goes in **my** garage.
Thanks, Miss Storm! Cool!
Like you need a car. This city's seen enough excitement for one day!
The Enc